I'm Going To READ!

These levels are meant only as guides;
you and your child can best choose a book that's right.

Level 1: Kindergarten–Grade 1 . . . Ages 4–6
- word bank to highlight new words
- consistent placement of text to promote readability
- easy words and phrases
- simple sentences build to make simple stories
- art and design help new readers decode text

Level 2: Grade 1 . . . Ages 6–7
- word bank to highlight new words
- rhyming texts introduced
- more difficult words, but vocabulary is still limited
- longer sentences and longer stories
- designed for easy readability

Level 3: Grade 2 . . . Ages 7–8
- richer vocabulary of up to 200 different words
- varied sentence structure
- high-interest stories with longer plots
- designed to promote independent reading

Level 4: Grades 3 and up . . . Ages 8 and up
- richer vocabulary of more than 300 different words
- short chapters, multiple stories, or poems
- more complex plots for the newly independent reader
- emphasis on reading for meaning

LEVEL 3

STERLING CHILDREN'S BOOKS
New York

An Imprint of Sterling Publishing Co., Inc.
1166 Avenue of the Americas
New York, NY 10036

Lot: 20 19 18 17 16 15 14 13 12   01/19

Published by Sterling Publishing Co., Inc.
1166 Avenue of the Americas, New York, NY 10036
Text © 2008 by Harriet Ziefert, Inc.
Illustrations © 2008 by Lee Wildish
Distributed in Canada by Sterling Publishing
c/o Canadian Manda Group, 664 Annette Street,
Toronto, Ontario, Canada M6S 2C8
Distributed in the United Kingdom by GMC Distribution Services,
Castle Place, 166 High Street, Lewes, East Sussex, England BN7 1XU
Distributed in Australia by NewSouth Books University of New South Wales,
Sydney NSW 2052, Australia

I'm Going To Read is a trademark of Sterling Publishing Co., Inc.

Library of Congress Cataloging-in-Publication Data

Wildish, Lee.
  The boy who cried wolf / pictures by Lee Wildish.
    p. cm.—(I'm going to read)
  "Text copyright 2008 by Harriet Ziefert, Inc."
  ISBN-13: 978-1-4027-5546-0
  ISBN-10: 1-4027-5546-5
  [1. Fables. 2. Folklore.] I. Harriet Ziefert, Inc. II. Title.

PZ8.2.W65Boy 2008
398.2—dc22
[E]

                                                    2007029925

ISBN: 978-1-4027-5546-0

For information about custom editions, special sales, premium and
corporate purchases, please contact Sterling Special Sales
Department at 800-805-5489 or specialsales@sterlingpublishing.com.

The Boy Who Cried WOLF

Pictures by Lee Wildish

STERLING CHILDREN'S BOOKS
New York

This is Tom.
His father is a shepherd.

Tom watches the sheep
when he is not in school.

One day, Tom decided
to have a little fun.

He yelled, "A wolf is trying
to eat our sheep!"

Three hikers heard his cry.
"Don't worry," said the first hiker.
"Don't be afraid," said the second.
"Where's the wolf?" asked the third.

Tom pointed to the trees.
"He's over there," he said.

The hikers looked
high and low for the wolf.

Finally, they shouted,

"THERE IS NO WOLF!"

Tom laughed and said,
"You're right.
I fooled you.
There is no wolf."

Before the hikers went back
into the woods, they said,
"You will not fool us again.
Not ever."

On a different day when
Tom was watching the sheep,
he saw three fishermen
down by the lake.

He yelled,
"A wolf is trying
to eat our sheep!"

The fishermen heard his cry.
"Don't worry," said the first fisherman.

"Don't be afraid,"
said the second.

"Where's the wolf?"
asked the third.

Tom pointed toward the woods.
"He's over there," he said.

The fishermen looked
high and low for the wolf.
Finally, they shouted,

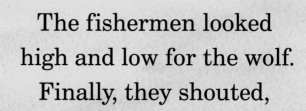

"THERE IS NO WOLF!"

Tom laughed and said,
"You're right. I fooled you.
There is no wolf."

Before the fishermen went back
to the lake, they said,
"You will not fool us again.
Not ever."

One day while Tom was
watching the sheep,
a real wolf came out of the woods.

Tom yelled,
"A wolf is trying
to eat our sheep!"

The hikers heard him.
"There is no wolf," they said.

The fishermen heard him.
"There is no wolf," they said.

They all thought Tom was
trying to fool them,
so they didn't run to help.

That night, Tom's mother and father
were ready to have dinner.
Tom was not there.

"Where is he?" they asked.

They found Tom outside.
"What happened?" they asked.

"A wolf came and chased
away the sheep," Tom said.
"Nobody came when I yelled."

Tom walked home
with his mom and dad.

"I believe you," said his father.
"I believe you," said his mother.

"Tomorrow we will
look for the sheep."

"But from now on,
if you want others to believe you,
you should always tell the truth."